HECTOR PROTECTOR
AND
AS I WENT OVER THE WATER

HECTOR PROTECTOR
AND
AS I WENT OVER THE WATER

TWO NURSERY RHYMES WITH PICTURES
BY
MAURICE SENDAK

MACMILLAN

Copyright © 1965 by Maurice Sendak

ISBN 0 333 37148 8

First published by Harper and Row, Publishers, Inc., 1965
First published in Great Britain by The Bodley Head Ltd., 1967
Picturemac edition published 1984

Printed in Hong Kong

Hector Protector was dressed all in green.

Hector Protector was sent to the queen.

The queen did not like him

no more did the king

so Hector Protector was sent back again.

As I went over the water

the water went over me.

I saw two little blackbirds sitting on a tree.

One called me a rascal

and one called me a thief.

I took up my little black stick

and knocked out all their teeth !

The youngest of three children, Maurice Sendak was born in Brooklyn in 1928. There was never any doubt of what he wanted to do: 'My brother Jack was always illustrating – so I copied him. We were always making up books together.' He finds illustrating, and writing, children's books the most challenging form of artistic expression, and in this field he has made himself a byword. In 1964 *Where the Wild Things Are* won him the Caldecott Medal, the American Library Association's award for the most distinguished picture book of the year; and in 1970 he received the Hans Christian Andersen Illustrator's Medal – the highest international honour in children's books. His latest and most long-cherished venture is to illustrate a collection of Grimm fairy tales, *The Juniper Tree* (translation by Lore Segal and Randall Jarrell), published in 1974.

Other Picturemacs you will enjoy

Tim's Last Voyage   Edward Ardizzone
Herself and Janet Reachfar   Jane Duncan
Janet Reachfar and Chickabird   Jane Duncan
Claire's Secret Ambition   Charlotte Firmin
The Girl who Loved Wild Horses   Paul Goble
The Gift of the Sacred Dog   Paul Goble
A Kindle of Kittens   Rumer Godden
The Old Woman who Lived in a Vinegar Bottle   Rumer Godden
Creepy Castle   John Goodall
Jacko   John Goodall
The Midnight Adventures of Kelly, Dot, and Esmeralda   John Goodall
Naughty Nancy the Bad Bridesmaid   John Goodall
Paddy's Evening Out   John Goodall
Shrewbettina's Birthday   John Goodall
The Surprise Picnic   John Goodall
Chocolate Mouse and Sugar Pig   Irina Hale
Donkey's Dreadful Day   Irina Hale
Beauty and the Beast   Rosemary Harris/Errol Le Cain
Maybe it's a Tiger   Kathleen Hersom/Niki Daly
Oh Lord!   Ron and Atie van der Meer
Peace at Last   Jill Murphy
On the Way Home   Jill Murphy

The Church Mice books by Graham Oakley

The Church Mouse   The Church Mice Adrift
The Church Cat Abroad   The Church Mice at Bay
The Church Mice and the Moon   The Church Mice at Christmas
The Church Mice Spread their Wings   The Church Mice in Action

also by Graham Oakley   Hetty and Harriet